MOUNT TAHLUL

MOUNT TAHLUL
TALES OF THE MOUNTAINS

Muhammad Ali Alwan

Translated from Arabic by
Abdulrahman Jones

MOUNT TAHLUL
TALES OF THE MOUNTAINS

Muhammad Ali Alwan

Published by Nomad Publishing in 2023
Email: info@nomad-publishing.com
www.nomad-publishing.com

Cover design: Lucie Wimetz

ISBN 9781914325489

The Publishers would like
to thank the Harf Literary Agency

Printed in India by Imprint Press

To one of these mountains, I dedicate these tales.

To my father, teacher and

friend Ali Muhammad Alwan,

who will not read it.

Time, once deemed a loyal mate of old,
Causes us pain with its grip, so cold.
The burden must be borne by all who live,
though some may taste the pleasure it gives.

Al-Mutanabbi

In a solitary room, a ring sits near a lamp, which casts a muted glow. A palpable stillness envelopes the space, suffocating any sound that dares to rise. Yet, in this eerie hush, a hand silently appears, dimming the ring's feeble glow. Suddenly, the lamp flickers and goes out, plunging the room into an impenetrable darkness.

In this abyssal absence of light, even the eyes lose their power of sight.

The widow and her three daughters are now imprisoned within the four walls of their home, their existence confined to a solitary space, where the only beginning is an oppressive silence.

Beit min Lahm, by Yusuf Idris.

MOUNT TAHLUL
Tales of the Mountains

S tories of mountains cannot be erased by the hand of time. They may fade in the memories of, or hide their tales from, the people born and raised on their slopes or in their shadow, but the mountains, their trees and deep valleys only grow and flourish.

Every mountain has its own unique story. The higher it rises, penetrating the clouds, the more it can hide its secrets and conceal its stories.

Villages that are scattered between the mountains and along the valleys, are places of songs – sung on farms and by wells, from daybreak till dusk – love stories, and lovers' trysts long gone.

Singing was their daily bread, not like in the cities, where people are trapped in houses and singing is not as appreciated like it is in the villages, where stories, songs and even laughter or a simple anecdote move easily across rooftops, as if carried by the breeze and dispersed among the clouds, trees and rushing currents.

Walking across the mountain on dark nights is a risky venture. It makes the heart surrender to doubt. The body is frightened to the core. The heart beats faster as one tries to catch a glimpse of sanctuary but cannot see or hear anything apart from the random sound of the wind in the trees.

Mount Tahlul has its own tales, the human stories of hearts broken by life's adversaries, unemployment and drought, and tales of the tribe of jinn that inhabited the mountain, which would emerge on the darkest nights and scare the traveller on his horse or donkey. On the moonlit nights, the jinn would stay away.

Mount Tahlul decided to reveal its secrets and recite them

every morning on a cloudy day, to the flocks of white clouds.

Tahlul is the memory of those who once wandered beneath the trees, burdened by the struggles of life and seeking a way out of poverty in their villages, which offered little beyond mere survival. These villages had long been forsaken by rain, leaving the land and its inhabitants parched.

Legend has it that Tahlul is home to a tribe of jinn, who have dwelt there since ancient times. Although the jinn are seldom felt during daylight hours, the night is their time to be active. Travelling on the mountain at night can be a harrowing experience, as the rider may be subjected to strange images, and eerie and alien voices that can induce panic. On the other hand, the white nights, illuminated by moonlight, provide a sense of security and reveal the paths, trees, and plateaus where the jinn stay for three consecutive nights.

Tahlul is a steadfast companion to the clouds, keeping the stories of those who have passed by. Each person has a story to tell, but many are reluctant to share their experiences for fear of reprisal from the mountain's mysterious inhabitants.

From a distance, Tahlul seems like a watchful guardian, opening a door to the sunset and bidding farewell to the sun as it disappears into the sea to prepare for the next day. This mountain is the subject of many tales, though the truth has become a semi-myth in the minds of travellers, particularly during the dark, merciless winter nights.

As I approached the city, the wide gates loomed before me. I had come from the southwest, where the salty sea air and the mist from the tall mountains still clung to my shoulders. The only trace of the sea birds was their distant calls that came and went in waves, as I trudged through the sandy desert with my eyes tightly shut. The winds shifted and the landscape changed, adding to the sense of disorientation that had been slowly creeping up on me.

Despite my efforts to keep it at bay, the feeling of being a stranger in this place invaded me. I swallowed hard, my throat tight with emotion, and fought back tears. Gritting my teeth, I willed myself to keep going, to push through the overwhelming emotions. Finally, after swallowing my saliva for the fourth and final time, the wave of tears receded.

At that moment, I decided to embark on a journey without hesitation or second thoughts. This is how I operate in all aspects of life - I make a choice and then either succeed through adaptation or accept defeat.

As I travelled, the sea appeared to be receding into the distance, the waves breaking and disappearing into the blue horizon as I ascended the mountain. It felt as though the sea was waving goodbye to me through the motion of the waves.

On the journey, the taxi driver abruptly stopped and turned off the engine. He then examined each passenger's face before we understood his intentions and retrieved our money from our pockets. With the money in hand, the taxi driver restarted the engine and navigated the bumpy dirt road.

I recalled some advice to not converse with those who refuse to meet your gaze. Despite my efforts to speak to them, they kept their eyes forward and remained unresponsive. The dust barrier seemed impenetrable, but I held on and enjoyed the peace of the silence, reassuring myself that it would eventually dissipate.

As I persevered, I clung to the thought that my love would endure forever. I reached for my bottle of Paris Blue Nights perfume, which remained untouched and full of scent.

As her gentle hand rested on my shoulder, she softly suggested, "Why don't you take a coat or winter clothes?" Her words pierced my heart, and I suddenly realised how far I would be from the mountains and my mother's face. I nodded my head and grabbed a winter coat that I rarely wore.

I avoided meeting her gaze, instead focusing on my father's gun hanging on the wall.

The radio was draped in embroidered cloth to protect it from dust.

I left our home after kissing my mother's hands and forehead, the fragrance of henna in her hair lingering in my memory. As usual, she insisted on seeing me off and kissed my closed eyes, and I departed as if I didn't know the path I had taken hundreds of times before.

When I left the mountain, it stood alone, overwhelmed by the view of the sea and distant mountains. I muttered to myself, "The city will conquer it one day." For it was the first step when dust began to take hold that engulfed the towering buildings and swirled up papers and discarded newspapers that readers were tired of due to their predictable and repulsive content.

On a Thursday, I arrived at my office only to realise it was an official holiday. The silence was deafening, and the absence of my colleagues only amplified it. I noticed a significant backlog of transactions from Wednesday. It was ten in the morning, and my immediate desire was to make myself a cup of tea. For the next hour, I was the only one present in the office, diligently working through the pile of work.

As I was nearing the end of my tasks, I decided to pay a visit to the manager, who was on the upper floor. After exchanging greetings, he gestured for me to sit down, and I obliged.

He seemed preoccupied, and his sadness was palpable. He then dropped the bombshell: "Do you know what happened?"

I said: "Communication failed, didn't it?" trying to sound very confident.

His eyes lingered on me for a moment before continuing in a tone full of pain, "The Iraqis have conquered Kuwait."

I was stunned into silence and quickly made my exit from his office.

Upon reaching my office, I shut the door and took a moment to process the news. By the time the noon prayer had ended, I could no longer bear the weight of my thoughts and decided to visit my regular cafe. I ordered a cup of tea, anxiously waiting for the news bulletin, but nothing came. I felt a sense of bitterness consuming me, and as I got on my car, I turned on the radio, hoping for any news update, but to no avail.

I found myself standing dazed outside a dear friend's house. His wife's voice rang out, inquiring about the identity of the visitor at the door, and I couldn't help but blurt out, "Saddam!" Her stifled laughter was filled with melancholy.

When the door finally opened and I saw him. I was greeted by a reflection of myself in the mirror, surrounded by a cloud of translucent sadness and bitterness.

It was at that moment that I knew something was amiss, a memory stirring from a dream that had been filled with love, literature and a longing for a broader horizon. We ate lunch with a heavy cloud of worry hanging over our heads, tears threatening to spill over but never quite making it out of our hearts.

Like a wave crashing against the shores of the future, the realisation hit me that my mother, father, and brothers were far away, and I was all alone, gripped by the fear of impending danger.

My grandmother's words echoed in my mind like a

prophecy told hundreds of times: "A war in Iraq, may God protect you from such evil." The illuminated billboards and road signs disappeared, replaced by this ominous phrase that seemed etched on every face I encountered.

As night fell, everything seemed to take on a different size; everything, including emotions.

Upon arriving in Basra, I was struck by the sight of palm trees stretching out before me, a moment of forgiveness washing over me. I immersed myself in the features of domestic faces, the bustling hotels and popular cafes, taking solace in the familiar Iraqi dialect and the sight of women's black coverings.

Their joyous laughter echoed through the air, a sound born from hearts that held deep reverence for the palm fronds and the flowing rivers and streams that had existed since ancient times.

I approached the south, how similar it was!

I found myself sitting beside a man who sipped tea

delicately from a small plate after pouring it into the cup of tea, taking in the serene surroundings. When he turned to me with a gentle expression, I summoned the courage to ask, "Do you know the village of Sayyab?" He smiled, and after taking a cigarette from his upper pocket, he passed his tongue over it before lighting it with a match. As he exhaled a deep breath, he pointed to the distance and said, "There is an old tailor there, who I know and used to visit." Overwhelmed with gratitude, I thanked him wholeheartedly.

I knew the village wasn't far away, and my friend was encouraging me to go there, but I didn't say anything and just told him decisively that we should head back to the hotel. He understood what I meant. I wanted to hold onto the dream as I knew and read about, and my friend could sense that.

As we travelled back to Kuwait, dust accompanied us, but the vibrant green colour of the palm trees and the joyous laughter of women in their abayas remained imprinted in my heart.

He scanned around the little house, taking in the sight of the worn-out windows and walls that had lost their once-white colour to the relentless passage of time. As he looked at the wrinkles etched on his mother's face that he loves, he glanced back at the old radio and the gun resting on the table, holding its cold iron in his hand.

Although he didn't know his father very well, his mother had instilled within him a deep love and admiration for that tall man who was a relentless fighter.

One day, he asked his mother, "Who was he fighting against?" She turned to him with an astonished look, as if the question was almost blasphemous. Her eyes flashed with a cloud of sudden anger, and then she calmed down a little as she replied, "The family of so-and-so, and the family of so-and-so." He said in astonishment: "But they were kin!!" Silence took over, and her forehead furrowed in sadness. And through her small mouth, she said: "They were true men, true men indeed" with a clear hint of pride, her eyes gazing off into the distance.

"Your father was the only one in the village who knew how to read and write," she continued. "He had a voice that exuded manliness and a youth that drew attention. He couldn't tolerate injustice."

As she spoke, she drew a deep sigh from inside her and shook her slender body, lost in the memories that gave her face the glow of sincere love. "At the end of the night, he used to talk to me about his childhood. He loved to remind me of the village, and always talked about our wedding night. I listened as if he was telling me something new. Every time he told me the story, I remember how I extended my hand with a cup of bitter coffee, and how the warmth of his fingers touching mine made my heart jump out of its place, wanting to kiss his forehead, his eyes... and his mouth that dripped sweetness and memories."

He turned to me once and said, "Do you remember the hairdresser?" I closed my eyes and transported back in time to my wedding day. I remembered the brunette hairdresser combing my hair, filling it with perfume, and weaving in basil branches with black and white flowers, crowned with their green colour my long, charred hair. I recalled tucking the caddis plant into my chest under my wedding clothes, the scent of it filling the air. I closed my eyes in fear and shyness.

I opened my eyes and saw my aunts nearby, carefully arranging whatever clothes my father had bought for me in the medium iron-coloured bag with its simple drawings in many colours. I had looked at it many times and it had stayed in my imagination till this very moment.

The men were scattered about, each of them participating in the night of the wedding with dancing and singing. The fires on the roof of the house were almost extinguished, so they kneaded ash balls with kerosene and placed them on the edges and sides of the roof, igniting them once again. Everyone's faces were alight with joy and singing.

Suddenly, she fell silent, a breath-taking stillness emanating from her as if she was recalling those flames and the accompanying joy of that moment that could never be recovered. It fainted like the lamps of modern weddings, void of truth and love.

Her face transformed into a strange smile, which quickly dissipated as she pursed her lips and entered a world of silence that I respected.

"Why were you smiling just now?"

She turned to face me: "Memories of your father flooded my mind, and I caught a glimpse of the hairdresser behind me, carrying a small chair, which I rested on every now and then. We were making our way to your father's house, which wasn't too far away, considering how small the village was."

The wedding procession moved ever so slowly. Women performed ululations, especially the dark-skinned ones. The hairdresser continued to do her job, stubbornly setting the chair down for me to rest on between each step. As I sat down, she took a moment to adjust my hair, straighten the edges of my wedding dress, and reveal my feet with their henna tattoos. She searched for ways to prolong my time on the chair.

Meanwhile, I sat there stealing shy glances at your father's face. I could feel his disapproval, but also a sense of resignation as he tried to adhere to the traditions of our society.

Despite his anger, I smiled inwardly, feeling lucky that he wasn't like the others. I closed my eyes, savouring the joy that was to come, a dream filled with surprises.

Your father was dressed in a pure white outfit, with a shaman robe adorning his midsection. His long black hair fell over his shoulders, and he had a Yemeni quilt draped over them. I knew the quilt must have been precious and expensive, but I couldn't help the grin that spread across my face as we approached the house's gate. One of my aunts whispered in my ear, "Don't be deceived by this joy and forget your place. Let him put his quilt on the floor opposite the door." I felt a wave of mercy wash over me, and as I looked into your father's eyes, I saw a word silently spoken: "Enough." I almost bowed to him, but my mother's sharp pinch in my waist brought me back to reality.

Trembling and unsure, I spoke up in a shy and neutral voice,

"I swear to God, I won't enter your house until you place your quilt under my feet." Ululations filled the air as I made my demand. Your father was stubborn and turned to his brothers. I feared another pinch from my mother as I waited for his response. Suddenly, he removed his quilt when the hairdresser shouted, "Get up, it's over!" Feet multiplied, ululations erupted in a crazy demonstration of joy, and when I crossed the threshold of the door, hundreds of bullets were fired in celebration.

All that he could hear now was his mother's heartbeat. His mother's face lit up with love and joy. He watched her talking, with pure joy. I sensed her ability to capture every detail, every person's face, men and women. This kind of limitless joy invaded my heart.

As he sat in the quiet of his room, his gaze wandered unconsciously to the old radio. At this moment he felt his mother's tone change. She started to use harsh tones to describe his father's voice.

In his mind's eye, he saw his father sitting in front of the dying embers of the fire in the hall. His father was a stern man, with sharp features and an unwavering gaze. He was recounting stories of his travels to the distant mountains, regaling his son with tales of jinn and manhood. His mother sat beside him, lost in her own thoughts.

He noticed his mother lost in the silence of her memories. Suddenly, the old radio sprang to life, and he imagined his father's voice emanating from it. He closed his eyes and conjured up an image of his father's youthful and vibrant face. And there was his mother giving him his cup of coffee with inherent love and respect.

Memories seemed to cloud around my mother, enveloping her in a halo of light. As I listened to my father's voice coming out of the radio, I couldn't help but observe my mother's emotions. I listened to their speech: my father sent me on a journey to Abha, a far-off village that was a world away from the familiar alleys, winding roads, and comforting smells of our own village of Tuhamia.

My father instructed me saying: "Go and deliver this message to your cousin and return without waiting for a response." With a smile, his father encouraged him in the first test of manhood and patience. In that moment, he understood how a person grew; it was like juniper trees that live for a long time.

The frigid chill penetrated my bones, as a man from Tuhama accustomed to warmth, but here I stood in the unforgiving mountains of Al-Suda.

The sun was only minutes away from setting, and after a gruelling seven-hour uphill trek to Tahalal, I finally arrived. A small, sharp knife and a baton that terrified even the jinn were tucked in my belt. The biting cold of Al-Suda showed no mercy to outsiders, as my teeth chattered uncontrollably.

With trembling hands, I performed ablution, the icy water only intensifying the unrelenting cold. I sought shelter in a small mosque. The warm breath of the visitors, and the weighty woollen clothes they donned provided some respite from the frigid air. The light of the lantern flickered, casting strange shadows on the worshipers' faces that I could scarcely make out.

After the prayer was concluded, the sound of voices mixed with the sweet melodies of praise and forgiveness filled the air, then ebbed away, leaving a sudden calm in the mosque. People began to leave one by one, their voices praising the name of God as they left through the door.

As I stood there, a gentle voice broke the silence, whispering to me, "My son, it seems you are a stranger to this village." I nodded in agreement.

He said, "Pray the Sunnah and then we'll see what good can we do for you."

I performed the Sunnah prayer and awaited the stranger's return outside the mosque. He appeared, draped in a quilt, and motioned for me to follow him. I obeyed.

As I followed my host into his stone abode, the warmth welcomed me with open arms. I took a seat in the spacious guest room, keeping a respectful distance. As I surveyed my surroundings, my eyes were drawn to the various rifles adorning the walls, each with its own story to tell. To the front, a distinctive rose-coloured mattress flanked by two high pillows, reserved for a special guest, perhaps, caught my attention.

The owner of the house, a stranger whose name I did not know, welcomed me without prying into my affairs, granting me the grace of his hospitality. He repeated his welcome twice more before a hush settled in the room, and I knew it was my turn to speak.

His solemn face and white beard exuded a sense of trust, and his eyes were full of friendliness. He said, "A stranger's story is a treasure chest waiting to be opened."

He listened with rapt attention as I recounted my journey from its inception. He inquired about the weather, the prices of essential goods such as grain, honey, ghee and livestock, his experienced voice calm and collected.

"May God bless and guide you, my son," he said with authority and wisdom, leaving me with a sense of peace.

As the fragrant aroma of bread and meat wafted towards us, I realised the depth of my hunger. Suddenly, a short man with an unusual turban entered the room, and the owner of the house stood to greet him with reverence and respect. A sense of familiarity tickled the edges of my mind. However, I could not recall where I had seen him before, despite the mosque being quite small, and the fact that people in this village do not typically wear such turbans.

As the guest settled in the special seat, the rich aroma of freshly brewed coffee filled the room. They waited in silence until an old woman entered, the wife of the host, and welcomed us warmly. Despite the cordial greeting, I sensed a strange apprehension and tension in the air, but I managed to keep my composure and I focused on the unfolding events.

Suddenly, another voice greeted us, and I turned to see an old woman supporting a young girl, whose ethereal beauty was juxtaposed with her obvious weakness.

I turned my gaze away from her beautiful face and kept silent. I looked at the man in the turban, his eyes betraying a hidden desire that he tried to conceal. He began to recite some short verses from the Quran. I approached him until I was close, with a great sense of doubt beginning to weigh heavily on my mind. An uneasy silence permeated the room, and the man's muttering only added to the tension.

He placed his hand on the girl's shoulder and raised it to her face, his gaze becoming more intense and lustful. As his hand slipped down to her chest, I felt a surge of rage and disbelief. I didn't know exactly what happened, I only felt my hand connect with the man's cheek in a resounding slap.

At that moment, I realised the gravity of my mistake in regard to the gracious host who had welcomed and honoured me. I quickly sought to make amends for the precarious situation I had put myself in. With a firm grip on the man's neck, I proclaimed in a loud voice, shocking all who were present, "This man is a wanted criminal!"

The young woman fled the council with her relative, evidently in good health.

The homeowner remained calm despite my outburst, gently prying my hand from the man's collar. He said: "Calm down my son! Dinner is served, Let's eat first, and then you'll get what you want."

The dinner consisted of a spread of porridge, gravy, meat and hot grains and, though I was famished, the food felt heavy in my stomach like a leaden weight.

The room was filled with the aroma of basil and liquorice, which had spread over the bed made for me in a small room with only one window. I pulled the blanket over my head, then cast it aside. A sliver of light crept through the crack in the door, offering me some measure of comfort. I listened intently to the sound of footsteps outside my room, but soon they faded away and the light disappeared, leaving me alone with the eerie silence of the night.

The sound of the air outside gave the place a strange sense of solitude. I reflected on the events of the evening, feeling a slight smile curl at the corners of my lips. However, sleep would not come to me that night.

Soft knocks interrupted the stillness of the room, followed by the drowsy voice of the homeowner reminding me of the morning prayer at the mosque. After the prayer had ended, I approached him, and he regarded me with a long and contemplative gaze. "You may continue on your journey, my son," he said at last. I inquired about the wanted man, and the homeowner let out a deep sigh before responding, "You have freed us of him. We were relieved to discover that you were fast asleep."

I looked at him with gratitude and murmured, "You have my sincere thanks."

* * *

As the sun set over the western mountains, the night crept into Abha like a dark cloud, shrouding the city in an ominous veil. The once radiant sun transformed into a giant, orange ball, slowly sinking into the sea, signalling the arrival of a new, dark night, erasing the memories of the day from the pages of the calendar.

Every evening, the city came alive with the sounds of laughter and stories shared over dinner tables, as memories of the bustling al-Thuluth market and its colourful tales were recounted. Each household had its own unique history, and every girl carried a hidden story that remained concealed until revealed suddenly. Meanwhile, every boy boasted of daring adventures, some real, but many merely the products of their adolescent imaginations, inflated by the admiration of those who listened to them.

The al-Thuluth market was a bustling social place that drew people from far and wide, even as far as Tihama region. Families brought their various goods, including firewood, coal and a plethora of fruits and vegetables. Amid the hustle and bustle, the sound of prayers for sustenance and well-being echoed from within.

The market was bordered to the north by the Mnazir, Al-Badie', and Al-Ruba' neighbourhoods, while a crouching hill led westward to the Sea Square, where the police building and the Great Mosque stood tall. To the south lay the Municipal Building.

In the middle of al-Thuluth market was the infamous lantern post, which glimmered and illuminated the area with a circular light at night. However, during the day, the building took on a different appearance, because it bore a severed hand dangling from a wrist in a dark blue shade.

The scene was shocking, and even the market visitors avoided looking at it, but it was the law that was blindly applied without any explanation.

Bin Moftah Café was the only place that welcomed strangers from different villages and those without any relatives in Abha, as there were no restaurants. The concept was flawed, but there were some who opened their homes to these strangers for a small fee.

Hanash went down to the city of Abha, leaving his small village and his beloved Nalah, whom he had picked from all other girls of similar beauty and tenderness. However, Nalah was the only thing that shone the brightest during his wild nights, keeping him up chasing distant stars in the sky, and to whom he gave many names. But the most enchanting of them was the name he chose for her, Nalah, who became his obsession during the day, and a star in the skies of his heart at night.

He was overwhelmed by the sense of loneliness that filled him with countless thoughts that drove him to retreat into his own mind. Despite possessing a strong physique and striking masculine features, he often found himself grappling with conflicting ideas and emotions.

He entered the house of the single woman, who was old but had a generous face and smiled all the time, and had the ability to work and endure. She welcomed him and said, "Our lunch today is such and such, and a night in a private room alone costs four riyals. Do you have an animal?" He shook his head and said, with a slight embarrassed smile, "My legs are my only companion." She was suddenly overcome by memories of her youth, but quickly regained her composure and returned to her serious nature.

After welcoming him into her home, the woman prepared his room and carefully made his bed. She placed two sprigs of basil on his pillow, their fragrant scent filling the room. As she did so, memories of her late husband flooded her mind, causing her to feel sad and regretful. She closed her eyes and forced the thoughts from her mind, whispering a prayer to banish any negative influence. "May God curse Satan," she murmured before leaving the room.

"Your room is the second one on your right, and the washbasins are at the end of the corridor on the left." She didn't look back as she spoke, and only heard a soft "Thank you" in response.

As she returned to her own room, she caught her reflection in the mirror and couldn't help but notice the wrinkles that seemed to have appeared overnight. With a soft smile, she sought solace in prayer, hoping to banish any thoughts of vanity or despair.

Despite her concerns, her thoughts remained focused on the stranger who now shared her home. She had welcomed hundreds of guests before, but had soon forgotten their faces. However, this stranger was different. He carried a certain air of mystery, with eyes that seemed to hold a thousand untold stories. Handsome though he was, there was something burdening him, and she could not help but be curious about it.

She remarked to him, "Your eyes, my son, tell a tale of either a thief or a lover." He remained silent and turned his face away, afraid to meet her gaze.

She saw his confusion, sadness and retreat into silence. She regretted her harsh words and spent a sleepless night thinking about him.

She cried tears of reminiscence for the love of her past years, as she served strangers in her old age, always full of sighs. She sensed that this stranger had a story to tell, perhaps she could deduce it from his behaviour and experiences in life.

The following morning, Hanash woke up early and left his room. She greeted him with a warm morning salutation, and he responded in a voice she hardly recognised. She said, "I prepared a delicious breakfast." He glanced at her surreptitiously, as she added, "I made Arika soaked in ghee and honey for breakfast. I hope you enjoy it."

He nodded his head, thanking her for her kindness. She almost wanted to tell him that the meal wasn't included in the rent, but was afraid of how he might perceive her, so she remained silent.

Throughout the day, he was preoccupied with thoughts of his girlfriend and village. Nalah was taking up all his thoughts. He wondered if there was a way for him to be with her, but he knew that only the Almighty knew the answer. He recalled how she warned him about the city and its people, expressing her fear that he might fall in love with the city's ways and forget about his village and its simple, kind people. She warned him that the city could be like a monster that could change a person's nature and destroy their rural goodness.

He scrutinised the woman carefully, and reassured her, "Don't worry, your friend is a lion." She responded with a sly grin, "A lion? Or a Hanash (snake)..." He couldn't help but laugh from the depths of his heart and replied, "Both."

Hanash sat in the Ben Moftah Café, lost in memories of Nalah as he sipped his tea. A fellow café patron caught his eye and smiled at him intermittently, but Hanash's thoughts kept drifting back to Nalah. He recalled their last encounter when he asked her about the origin of her name. She simply shrugged and explained, "I don't know why my name is Nalah, but my father was a blacksmith who made axes for firewood, and there was a town in the south of our village called Tahlul. At the highest peak, they extracted iron from rocks that were struck by lightning, which never weaken. The name of that site is Ras Al-Naila. When I was born and when I cried, it was as if the sound broke through the darkness and made them feel my presence." My father said, "I'll name her Nalah," A name chosen by God in the heavens.

* * *

Al-Shaafi's shop was situated near the municipal building, east of the generator powering a few electric bulbs in the narrow alleys near the market. Constructed from adobe, the shop featured a sturdy double door made of juniper wood, secured with metalwork made in Germany.

Although not large in size, Al-Shaafi's shop held a plethora of precious items, including gold and silver belts, priceless jewellery for women, and a range of fabrics.

On Tuesdays, the shop bustled with patrons from nearby villages, men and women alike, each offering their goods for sale, meandering through the market's various shops.

Hanash left his home at Al-Ma'azbah's house and mingled with the people at Al-Thuluth Market. He did not know how fate led him to Al-Shaafi's shop. Standing at the door, he hesitated to enter, unsure of what to ask. The shop owner was dealing with some female shoppers inquiring about the prices of gold and silver belts, headbands and other accessories.

The sight of Nalah's unadorned wrists suddenly flashed in Hanash's mind, in this fleeting moment. As he stepped away from the shop's entrance, he was confronted by a lute, which sparked various thoughts and a momentary feeling of awe that quickly dissipated.

It was a pleasant and splendid Friday evening, despite it being at the beginning of the month, with the absence of the crescent moon making the night very dark. However, scattered lights at the entrances of neighbourhoods, coming from the municipality's generator and Ali bin Hassan's electric lamps, cut through the darkness and guided the passers-by to their destinations.

Shortly before the dawn call to prayer, a night watchman, who was roaming the centre of Abha, especially around its shops overlooking the market, arrived near Al-Shaafi's shop. He wore an olive coat and a dark green ghutra, and his palms felt cold as he touched the locks of closed shops. His face was tanned.

He felt suspicion as he headed towards the municipality's generator and Al-Shaafi's shop. As he approached the shop, he noticed an opening in the side of the building, allowing someone to enter. He couldn't control himself and started blowing his hoarse-sounding whistle loudly, like his chest was filled with the rattle from traces of cigarettes.

He ran frantically, blowing the whistle hysterically.

The police station was not far from the event, and circles began to form little by little, as the police guards heard the whistle and repeated the action. A group of soldiers rushed down to the centre of the market and towards Al-Shaafi's shop.

The soldiers did nothing, waiting long for orders from higher-ups before they took action.

When a low-ranking officer finally arrived on the scene, he warned the soldiers not to enter the shop and instructed them to avoid disturbing any potential evidence within a defined circle. As the call to prayer sounded, the news of the theft spread throughout Abha and the surrounding neighbourhoods. People gathered around the scene as soldiers secured the area and a higher-ranking officer, accompanied by a civilian officer, divided the crowds. From their whispered conversation, one phrase stood out: "He is as cunning as the devil, having hidden any evidence with an infernal plan." The thief had apparently spread out a cloth to transport the stolen goods, which he then discarded before disappearing from sight.

After the incident, the city of Abha became desolate at night, as no one knew who was responsible for the theft. Parents warned their families to stay indoors, and evening visits with neighbours were forbidden for a while, due to the fear of an unknown thief.

The feeling of apprehension continued to grow in the city, and questions were directed towards those responsible for the safety of the citizens. People became increasingly cautious when venturing out to neighbouring villages, and strangers were viewed with suspicion.

The police investigated numerous suspects, but none were convicted. The elusive thief became the topic of gossip in households, with rumours circulating about his physical and psychological traits, and his extraordinary feats. This generated information that even the police did not have, leading to confusion among officials. The lack of truth gave rise to illusions and assumptions that were far from reality.

Meanwhile, in the market of Mahail, about 120 km away from Abha, some indications began to emerge, but without confirmation. The journey to this distant location was arduous and could only be undertaken by animals or camels that could endure the rugged, rocky terrain and mountain descents. The valleys along the way often surprised travellers with sudden torrents from areas hundreds of kilometres away.

There were reports that a gold merchant from Mahail was offered a golden belt at a suspiciously low price by a Sirawy man. When the shopkeeper hesitated and asked questions, the Sirawy man suddenly disappeared without a trace. This sparked doubts and extended the circle of suspicion, but there was no sign of the belt's owner, as if he had vanished into thin air.

Once news spread among the people, the merchant became a prime target for the police and their endless investigations.

Interestingly, the owner of the store did not provide any information that could lead investigators to any breakthroughs. He simply said: "A young man with sharp features and an intimidating physique came to my store and offered a feminine belt made of gold. I estimated the belt's value, but offered him half the price, and wanted to obtain a purchase bond. I felt his apparent confusion and hesitation, and he did not discuss the price with me or ask for an increase. When I deliberately turned my face away from him, the young man put the belt calmly in a black bag and whispered, 'This sale was not meant to be closed, goodbye' And then he vanished."

Furthermore, the shop owner's prosperity grew remarkably compared to other merchants, and that was due to the attention of various investigators who asked about the belt's owner. The owner denied knowing anything and stated that the young man was from the mountains that rose to the clouds in the west. When asked to describe the young man's features, the owner said: "He is a man of imposing stature, with a muscular build, stern countenance and eyes that strike fear into others. Despite his smooth facial features, his smile is filled with malice and sarcasm. He dons a thick black tunic that reaches his shoulders, giving him an intimidating presence. Wearing a traditional Syrian Jambiya, he walks with firm, unwavering steps, never looking back. Although I only caught a glimpse of him as he left my shop, his figure was quickly lost in the bustling crowd of the market, disappearing among the throngs of shoppers."

The investigators gathered their papers and notes before returning to the softness of the city. Pressure began to mount on them, causing confusion and disarray. Their eyes searched the villages secretly and greedily, hoping to find a trail to follow. Word had spread of a thief stealing sheep, but such thieves are many and they did not harm the people or the shepherds.

Each day, they return to their respective villages at sunset, taking the stolen sheep that were left unattended by the shepherd.

Their intuition led them to investigate the known sheep thieves, one by one, until they had narrowed it down to three suspects. They dismissed two, leaving only one who closely matched the description of the perpetrator. That's when Hanash appeared to them.

He realised that he was close to being arrested and used his cunning to evade his pursuers, including the sleepless eyes of the police, and the families that were driven by many desires including curiosity and revenge.

Nalah's heart was heavy as she waited for him, for what seemed like an eternity, hoping that he would fulfil her dreams, despite her unwavering love for him. She had always advised him to be patient and prudent, urging him to work towards a better future instead of indulging in reckless adventures, but her pleas had fallen on deaf ears.

He boasted of his bravery and physical prowess, valuing no one, and taking pleasure in repeating his wild exploits.

The memory of the day when she had met him, unintentionally, was etched in her mind with immense pain and sadness. She carried a water skin on her back and picked basil leaves for him, and the scent of henna clung to her palm. He nervously looked around, turning left and right, afraid of the watchful eyes. He took a bite of the basil, and for a moment, his beautiful smile shone on his face. However, as soon as he smelled the basil mixed with henna, his smile faded away, and his eyes welled up with tears, which he wiped away with the edge of his veil. He fled in a moment of weakness, leaving her alone, and went into the fields. That was the last time she saw him. She felt a lump in her throat that made it hard to shed tears. She was overwhelmed by a profound sadness that seemed to consume every part of her body, and a sense of doubt crept in. She had a strong feeling that something would happen to him or her family, but the future was unclear and shrouded in uncertainty.

As she entered her house, she took off her yellow scarf that covered her hair, threw it aside and emptied her water bottle into the large empty jar. She ran to her room to be alone, unable to face anyone, and as soon as she was there, her eyes overflowed with tears, but no sound escaped her lips.

As she sat in her room with its walls adorned with Al-Qatt paintings that broke the monotony of the white walls, Nalah recalled his words, spoken to her in the fields. He had said, "We all lie to improve our image, to deceive each other, and to paint a false picture of ourselves that we come to believe. Isn't that what life is about?" When she had raised her eyebrows in surprise, he had smiled and added, "Yes, we are all thieves, and we hide it even from ourselves."

His physical descriptions, as provided by the owner of the gold store, began to come into focus for the investigators, along with the name of his village and other information that led them to the deputy of his tribe. After weeks of careful searching and tracking, they discovered his name, his family name and his house. For a while, the house remained untouched, with no one entering or leaving, until one of the neighbours became suspicious of its deserted appearance, despite being habitable. The deputy was informed of the neighbour's suspicions, and word began to spread.

Ultimately, the younger brother of the deputy formed a group of strong and courageous men from the village to arrest him. On a cold and rainy night, they descended from the high mountains to the village, and the air grew even colder.

The besiegers of the house sensed suspicious movements coming from within. One of them knocked on the door and demanded to know if anyone was inside. The movements quieted, and after an hour of tedious waiting, the deputy's brother approached the locked door, introduced himself, and assured the person that if they surrendered, they would be safe wouldn't be mistreated.

After a short while, the group heard movement and a voice

from inside the house full of hope, saying "I am safe in the hands of God and now I entrust myself to your protection." The deputy's brother replied, "Fine. This is a gentleman's agreement," and retrieved a wooden key from under the door.

The deputy's brother took the key and attempted to open the door, but a gunshot struck his hand and arm, causing him to fall unconscious. The others rushed to his aid and called for someone from the health centre to help him.

Chaos erupted, and one of them entered the house, only to find it empty. After searching all the rooms, he discovered an open window in the back, through which the escapee had fled.

For an entire month, people scoured the village, fields, valleys and mountains to find the fugitive, but their efforts proved fruitless. They lost hope of catching him, and the deputy's brother, now healed but with his injured arm bound to his neck, harboured pent-up hatred. He declared that only one person could have pulled off such a feat and ran to his council, wondering silently, "Who could it be?" He informed them that this bold and cursed Hanash had a history of such deeds, but he was determined to defeat him, no matter how long it took. They nodded in agreement, resolved and defiant.

One morning, a farmer's wife brought him his breakfast of a wheat pie and a coffee pot full of water from the well. Two bulls were standing nearby, and the wife had brought them fodder.

As they conversed, the farmer noticed a man sneaking into the well. He signalled to his wife to remain calm and approached the well quietly. The man was drinking water from his palms, and the farmer shouted for help from the villagers. His wife joined him in screaming, and he pulled his sharp blade from his belt. Hanash continued to drink water quietly and realised he had been caught. The men rushed to the well, each carrying a weapon, and besieged it. Hanash surrendered by raising his arms upward, and the villagers handcuffed him and took him to the house of the representative's brother, who thanked them and praised their efforts.

Hanash was starving, so the representative ordered him to eat and drink. He said to him, "God's law will be our judge." Hanash ate quietly and didn't give any answer, he only thought of Nalah's bright face. Despite being at large, the security was tight, and most people were armed, but Hanash smiled sarcastically with a sense of condescension.

The following day, a group of men escorted him to Abha and through Jabal al-Safra, which led them to the city centre where the principality and the legal court were located. They chanted and danced as they travelled, but he only grinned and insulted them one by one with obscene words. He repeated, "I am only a weak thief, but you are like docile sheep who cower before the powerful."

They arrived at the municipal headquarters, where he was received and then transferred to prison to await his trial. Despite being behind bars, he shouted insults and incited the other prisoners to revolt, but they paid him no attention. When the authorities were informed, the Emir demanded an urgent trial to prevent any further disturbances.

The verdict was issued, and he confessed to the crime, stating that his trial was fair and that he was not coerced. As punishment, his hand was to be amputated.

Meanwhile, in the stillness of the night, a woman who had been unable to sleep started weeping again, which she had learned to suppress due to her old age and years of experience with the many people who came to her hostel. Unusually, she apologised for not receiving any guests for three days, mourning for Hanash, who had preoccupied her thoughts and stirred up her long-buried emotions, bringing back the excitement of life, while she reminisced about those days.

In the quiet village, Nalah could not sleep, as memories of him and their meetings in the fields and the well where she fetched water flooded her mind, causing her to weep throughout the night.

One Tuesday, his hand was severed and hung from the mast of the lantern post, serving as a warning to others. It was decided that the hand would remain there until Thursday, after which it would be taken down and buried in the nearest cemetery.

As expected, on Thursday three individuals went to complete the burial process. However, they were met with a shocking surprise when they approached the lantern post, only to find that it was no longer there. Hanash was spotted entering the infirmary to receive treatment, his gaze fixed on the Tuesday market. He descended from a red cart unassisted, a sarcastic smile on his lips.

Having been released from prison, he had nothing with him except for the clothes on his back - a state of utter destitution. Seeking refuge, he made his way to the Ben Moftah Café and ordered a cup of tea. The owner of the café, taking pity on him, offered him a kind gesture, "You are always welcome here, and you need not pay until you find employment. Then, you can become a regular customer."

Gratefulness was apparent on his face as he took a sip of tea - an experience that was made impossible due to his prior circumstances. A smile crept onto his face as he reminisced about the times when he used to frequent the coffee shop next to the police building, though they had failed to recognise him despite the passage of time.

The notion of visiting the single woman's house crossed his mind, even though he was aware that it would not reveal her love for him. However, the memory of Nalah and the possibility of being consumed by an incomplete experience dissuaded him, and he resolved to visit a different woman instead. With no money to his name and the sight of his severed hand too difficult to bear, he set off on his journey to the old woman.

As she welcomed him, an enigmatic tear trickled down her cheek, an expression of the unspoken love and compassion that she held for him.

"I really wish you would stay, and I'm happy to have you here, even if you don't pay," she said, her voice trembling with fear of his rejection. However, he entered into a world of silence, surrendering to the harsh reality.

That night, he slept for a long time, roused only by the

persistent knocking of the woman, who urged him to wake up. He made his way to the washroom, where he poured cold water over his body before dressing and donning his head cover. Inside the room, decorated with al-Qat al-Asiri and permeated with the scent of Javanese incense, he waited for the woman's arrival, feeling only the pangs of hunger. She finally entered with a large plate of Arika soaked in ghee and honey, place it in front of him and said with clear affection:

"Bon Appetit."

In a moment of forgetfulness, he withdrew his right hand from the sleeve of his dress, only to realise the extent of his loss. She stood before him, her hand covering her mouth, her eyes filled with a mixture of astonishment, pain and sorrow on his behalf.

As the sun rose, he bid her farewell, "Take care and keep well." He set out from the quiet city, bearing a grudge against the place that had robbed him of his hand.

* * *

All night long, I tried my best, both mentally and emotionally, to push the image of her out of my mind. She was on the verge of an inevitable end, and that image reminded me of burnt palm trees on a dusty day in Riyadh, at the beginning of each season. That scene now reminded me of her yellow face, devoid of any features. She came into my view feebly and slowly, with two eyes empty of any expression. At first, it seemed like she wanted to talk to me, to say something, to scream in my face as she used to when she was like a majestic palm tree, once heavy with dates. But she quickly shifted her gaze in another direction, in a weak and slow motion. Then I realised, from within, that things were moving forward and about to come to an end.

Suddenly, her cold eyes returned to me, as if signalling her desire to speak. Her lips trembled, but she didn't say a word. A long time passed, laden with multiple emotions of mercy, sorrow and sadness for what had become of things. I looked at her face, rich with wrinkles, and then her tongue came out, she wet her lips, and looked at me with cloudy focus. I could barely hear her weak and trembling voice asking for my name.

Her eyes fixated on my lips, as if that were a glimmer of hope for her, or the only thread of hope she clung to. Her desire was fixated on it, and it proved to her that the answer would dispel the clouds of lost memory. She shook her head many times, urging me to answer, before delving into her lost memory.

When she heard my name, which I repeated more than once, her eyes lit up with a sudden burst of life and she stole the glimpse of a smile from within the wrinkles. But then, the sadness and silence that had enveloped her since her stroke returned to her face. She realised that her ability to sequence events was no longer what it used to be, deep in the past, and that the faces she loved now answered her questions out of courtesy, leaving her exposed to the falsehood of their lies from time to time. All of this increased her sadness and loneliness in the house where she once was the shining star.

She raised her eyebrows and asked me to support her body that had become weak and exhausted from the passage of days and nights, and help her to her room. I remembered that moment, I remembered how I held her limp arm, feeling the bone and the sagging flesh, and the wrinkled veins that filled me with sorrow for this great woman. We were walking together to her small room, and I recalled her image from a long time ago when she came from Riyadh. My father told me about her strength and courage. When she came to us for the first time, I smelled a new fragrance that I had never smelled before. When I grew up, I learned that it was oud. She was tall and had a round face with two big, bold eyes that we were not used to seeing in my mother and her sisters. Does travel give a person this boldness? Does meeting others give them a different kind of courage from what is familiar? Her voice instilled fear in us, and we shuddered in real terror as our eyes conveyed it. She was a devout woman who knew many verses and hadiths, and extended her prayers noticeably. I would observe my mother praying, and I would find her prayer to be normal and rushed, whereas my aunt's prayer was lengthy and deliberate. Her authority did not confine itself only to me and my siblings, but extended to the symbol of the household, my father, who represented a huge mountain to us. I used to imagine him as Tahlul mountain, obscure and full of mysteries. He would stand before her like an innocent child, and perhaps that is what magnified her image in our minds; that image that knew neither compassion nor tenderness.

As she entered her room, her trembling fingers gestured for me to take a seat. Concerned she might suddenly fall, I sat close by. Slowly and deliberately, she withdrew a small key from the remnants of old clothes and fastened it around her neck. With a withered gaze, she pointed towards a small wooden box, black in colour, adorned with nails arranged in a distinct pattern, in a yellowish-copper hue. She lifted the box and leaned over it, attempting to open the lock several times, but failing due to her advanced age, trembling hands and weak eyesight. She looked at me with eyes full of despair and sorrow, swallowed hard with regret, pity and mercy for her condition, and the weakness that had taken over her after that dreadful stroke. In an attempt to speak to her as naturally and neutrally as possible, I offered, "Can I be of any assistance?" Suddenly, she spoke in a voice that I barely recognised as her own, asking, "Who are you?!" In response to her question, I spoke with the same natural and neutral tone, "I am your grandson, so-and-so." For a brief moment, I thought she recognised me, but she soon returned the key to its hiding place within her clothes. With her veined fingers, she gestured towards me, indicating that I should leave the room.

In a quiet voice, I asked, "Is there anything you need?" She stared at me for a prolonged moment, then closed her eyes.

Leaving the door slightly open, I exited the room.

As I made my way towards the family gathering, my mind was drawn back to that unforgettable day when she had lost her temper with one of my brothers, who had been particularly argumentative. Despite his behaviour, she had always stood by his side. However, on that occasion, her anger had boiled over, and she hit him with force. Unsatisfied with her initial outburst, she then proceeded to bite him, causing him to scream out in agony.

My father had entered the room, attempting to intervene and dissuade her from inflicting such a painful punishment upon my brother. However, her high-pitched and terrifying screams had drawn us all out of our rooms, with faces fixed on those two mountains; my father and grandmother.

We all watched the situation with faces etched with sadness and concern; my mother, brothers, sisters, aunt, and uncle - who lived with us under the same roof. Despite this gathering, she continued to scream relentlessly. My father tried to calmly reason with her, recounting his perspective for all to hear. Suddenly, she struck my father across the cheek with a powerful blow, prompting a deafening silence to fall upon the room. The sound of our racing hearts was almost audible, as we stood in stunned silence. Then, a sweet smile spread across my father's lips, and he took hold of her palm and kissed it repeatedly. Gazing upon us with an expression of command, he urged us to all to leave, and we wiped our tears as we left.

My grandmother only had my father and my aunt in terms of immediate family. Over the years, I travelled to various countries in both the east and west. However, there was a place in Tihama, with its mountains and valleys, where time seemed to stand still, and stories remained the same. The people, their faces, the beauty of the men, their sheep and cows, all remained constant in this vast hole surrounded by mountains on all sides. The sky above was covered with a transient blue veil that was occasionally adorned with clouds, lending a sense of change to the otherwise constant scenery to the inhabitants of this place, which they called home.

The houses were suspended over the slopes of the mountains, bearing witness to a previous era of prosperity. The caravans of merchants, with their many loads of goods, traversed the valley and headed towards this land. Merchants from other regions would also arrive to participate in weekly markets, making this a commercial and educational hub of great significance during those times. The multi-storey buildings, much like those seen today, were owned by groups of people.

Days passed slowly among the residents of this large village, with only the stories brought by the merchants to dispel the monotony of their routines.

One day, the villagers caught sight of a strange person for the first time. His complexion tended towards white with a hint of red, and his hair was markedly different from that of the local people. Moreover, his dialect was so unfamiliar that it was difficult for the locals to understand him when he spoke.

He rented a nice room with a small Arab bath in a house on the outskirts of the town. Whenever the women heard him speak in his foreign dialect, they would make jokes and gossip about him. They described his cheeks as being red like ripe tomatoes.

On the second day, everyone discovered that he was actually a doctor from the Ministry of Health, who had been sent by the Directorate to Abha to oversee the dispensary.

The dispensary's only clerk, elder Jaber, beamed with pride as he had now become an assistant to the doctor. However, he couldn't help but feel a sense of regret that his responsibilities were being taken away from him. From that moment on, he would no longer be able to prescribe headache pills or boast about his basic medical knowledge. He had been reduced to nothing more than an aide, waiting for the doctor to boil injections, sterilise wounds and clean the dispensary.

He harboured a hidden joy within him, for he intended to learn and emulate the doctor's profession. Like other doctors before him, he would only stay for a few months. When the hottest part of summer arrived and snakes slithered out of their burrows, he would tire of this monotonous life where there was nothing to see but these houses hanging on the slopes of high mountains, and when night fell heavily with loneliness and memories of their distant homelands, surely this doctor would not stay for long. He would be shocked by the extremely narrow-minded people who did not accept outsiders and only knew how to ridicule them to an astonishing degree. As if this pit they called a homeland had given them precise knowledge of everything, and each of them had a different name and title that only appeared when they were angry or mocking. No, this doctor would not stay for long.

However, something unexpected happened. The doctor became deeply involved in his work, taking his profession seriously and rarely cracking a smile. His dedication to the purpose of his profession – "saving others" - drove him to wake up early and head straight to the dispensary that elder Jaber had prepared. Over time, he began to warm up to the people of the village and during his leisure time, he would exchange stories with the locals. Elder Jaber would often ask him about his homeland, Syria, and his family, who he knew to be a prominent family in the city of Homs.

The doctor kept a small notebook with him and diligently wrote down the conditions of the people of the village, the nature of its people and their stories.

One day, elder Jaber asked him what he was writing. The doctor replied with a smile, "I write down the thoughts that cross my mind about myself and the people of this place." Elder Jaber felt a touch of joy, for it was the first time he saw the doctor smiling since he came to this village. That encouraged and prompted him to ask a sudden question, "Doctor, why don't you marry?" knowing that the doctor was single. The doctor smiled again and chuckled, his body shaking with laughter, and said to him, "Soon, God willing."

Elder Jaber asked: "From Sarwo or Tihama?" To which the doctor smiled a third time and asked back: "What's your opinion?" Elder jaber replied: "In my view, a Tihami girl is a better choice." At that moment, a patient entered and cut off their conversation.

The following day, the doctor arrived, and his primary concern was to meet elder Jaber. He found him in the dispensary with no patients at such an early hour. The doctor was eager to finish their talk about marriage, which elder Jaber had left open-ended. "Do you know of any family who would dare to marry off their daughter to a stranger?" Elder Jaber was taken aback by the question and began to ponder it carefully. "Who would agree to such a thing?" he asked himself. Even if the stranger was a doctor, the customs were strict, and people would aim their arrows of ridicule and mockery in every direction. Their tone of sarcasm and mockery spared no one, no matter who it was, and they knew the smallest details before the more important ones. In the village, nothing was hidden, and both men and women passed on information during their gatherings on the rooftops of their homes, or inside their houses during their late-night socialising.

Elder Jaber turned to the doctor and looked at his face, only to be met with a sudden explosion of emotion. "What's wrong with you, elder Jaber?" the doctor exclaimed, his voice rising in volume. Elder Jaber was taken aback and avoided looking directly at the doctor. "I was merely contemplating who would be worthy of being your wife, and you shout at me! You know what, I'll never do that again!" With that, elder Jaber quickly made his way out of the dispensary, heading towards his home, which was nearby. As he walked, he could hear the doctor's voice calling to him.

The doctor regretted his actions, particularly since Jaber was a highly respected elder among the people of the village. He spent considerable time pondering the situation and, upon leaving the infirmary, he did not return home. Instead, he decided to go to elder Jaber's house. A few moments after he knocked on the door, Jaber's wife welcomed him and invited him to join them for lunch. The doctor excused himself saying: "I need elder Jaber urgently." To which she replied: "Come in and share dinner with us for the sake of God."

He finally accepted the invitation and the smiling woman led him to the guest room. Elder Jaber himself returned after performing the Asr prayer, beaming with delight upon seeing the doctor. Elder Jaber's wife brought in a tray of coffee and dates, followed by a plate of Areka covered in honey and ghee that emitted a delightful fragrance. "Please, go ahead, Doctor, and forgive us for any shortcomings," she said graciously.

The doctor smiled warmly and replied, "No need for apologies, but indulging in this delicacy will raise my cholesterol to the highest level. May God bless you." Elder Jaber chimed in, "Walking is the key to burning off that excess cholesterol. And, Doctor, you are still young. May God grant you good health and wellbeing."

The doctor enjoyed the hospitality of elder Jaber and his

adoring wife. After sipping on his coffee, he thanked them for their kind gesture and hospitality before standing up to leave. As he bid farewell outside the house, he reminded elder Jaber of their conversation with a wink saying: "Don't forget our discussion." Elder Jaber replied confidently, "Everything will be alright, by the will of the Lord."

Time passed by without any significant change, except for the occasional visits to the small dispensary. It was a house rented from one of the well-off families in the village, consisting of a small pharmacy, dispensary, examination room, and a private room for the doctor to stay in. The room was modest, with a bed and a small cupboard containing a collection of medical books, and a multi-sided peg on which he hung all of his clothes. He felt encircled in this village, which was small and uneventful, except for the bi-weekly market in the neighbouring village. The market was a source of joy for the doctor, as he would get to see new faces and experience a sense of excitement.

Even the patients were the same. He could anticipate their needs and prescribe the right medication to help them heal, even without them telling him what they suffered from. The doctor had become intimately familiar with them, even memorising their names and funny nicknames that they disliked, especially from a stranger. They had an intense sensitivity and a fiery temperament that the rugged terrain of the high mountains had instilled in them. Their view of the sky was limited to a small opening through which they could glimpse the stars when the sky was clear, or the clouds drifting towards the sea.

In one of the forts nestled high in the mountains, towering above the valley floor, guarding itself from the powerful torrent that swept away anything in its path, sat Sharifa, decorating her delicate palms with henna and applying perfume to her forehead. Her beauty was all-consuming and set her apart from others her age. She gazed out of her small window at the turbulent movement of the torrent below, its waters still surging even after the successive rains had delivered their gifts to the earth, causing it to quiver and grow.

As she watched the water rushing by, a sigh escaped her chest, and for the first time, she thought about her future.

The next day, the sun rose, and the valley was filled with the scent of trees and plants after a joyous rainfall. The youth of the village sang songs of love, life, memories and grief, accompanied by the enchanting melodies of the Trouq. The girls listened attentively, feeling a sense of audacity as they eavesdropped on the singing through open windows.

In the village, stories about the marriage of the Syrian doctor started to circulate among the late-night gatherings, often accompanied by laughter from the women who enjoyed delving into the topic and inventing details that may or may not have been fictitious. It was the product of the imagination that characterised small, remote villages.

Sharifa cherished her older brother, who was a couple of years older than her, with all her heart, and was proud of him.

He had taught himself, served in the army for a number of years, and even travelled to Mecca and Medina, which the villagers referred to as Al-Sham. When he returned, she felt the warmth of his tenderness and protection towards her.

She was the only pampered child of her parents, and her body had matured, prompting her father to repeatedly inquire about her marriage plans. Whenever he asked, she would flee the scene, embarrassed. Her mother would smile and ask her husband not to repeat the question, which only served to further embarrass Sharifa. The father would chuckle and stroke his beard, which had turned grey with age, saying, "In the end, she will agree!"

Occasionally, she would contemplate the matter carefully as she observed her friends getting married to the village's youth or to the neighbouring villages' inhabitants. One of them had even married someone from Abha, a city known for its wealth, prestige, and bustling markets.

Sharifa had never been able to visit Abha, which was full

of captivating stories and well-known markets in all the nearby villages.

On Friday, just half an hour before prayer time, the doctor heard a knock on his door. He wondered who it could be and what they wanted, hoping it wasn't an emergency. Nevertheless, he didn't hesitate and opened the door, only to find elder Jaber standing there in his tidy clothes and expensive cloak. After exchanging pleasantries, elder Jaber told the doctor that he had some news to share but suggested that they pray first, and then discuss it. The doctor agreed, and they walked together to the mosque. Elder Jaber smiled and remarked, "I see you're wearing a garment like ours?" The doctor replied that it was more comfortable than trousers, especially during prayer.

After the prayer, the congregation dispersed and headed to their respective homes, with light raindrops bringing a sense of joy to their hearts and smiles to their faces. As they walked, elder Jaber turned to the doctor and said, "let's have lunch together?" The doctor tried to politely decline, but elder Jaber insisted, and the doctor couldn't help but wonder what news he had to share. So, he agreed and felt a strong curiosity brewing inside him.

As they enjoyed their coffee and tea after lunch, they gazed out of elder Jaber's window at the increasing rain. The valley below was filling up rapidly, with torrents rushing down from the mountains in the distance. As they continued to converse, elder Jaber made no reference to the idea of marriage that was occupying the young doctor's mind, instead giving a slight smile with a hint of mischief.

Elder Jaber's wife chuckled, interjecting, "Come on Jaber, tell the doctor what you have to say and give his mind a rest from all the worrying." Looking at her affectionately, elder Jaber responded, "All of Fatima's daughters like to rush things. But you know that marriage is like a dish that simmers quietly until it's fully cooked, right?" She nodded her head in agreement and excused herself from the gathering.

There was an awkward silence between them, and each of them hoped that the other would bring up the topic of marriage. If this marriage happened, it would be the first time such a marriage was taking place in this village and the surroundings. Elder Jaber finally turned to the doctor and, after several attempts, stuttered, "Doctor, I have no news for you." The doctor relaxed and replied, "Thank you, that's good to hear." Elder Jaber then remarked with a smile, "By God, Doctor, you have learned our dialect." The doctor responded, "Familiarity breeds contempt. I consider myself one of you now." To which elder Jaber replied, "Indeed, you are one of us."

Neither of them broached the subject of marriage, and when the doctor mentioned his upcoming annual leave, elder Jaber saw it as a chance to delay the matter until the doctor's return. It was also an opportunity to gather more information, including opinions from the chosen bride's family and the input of elder Jaber's wife, all to support making the right choice.

The sole doctor in the village had made the decision

to take his annual leave the following week. Meanwhile, another doctor had arrived to work at a dispensary located ten kilometres away in a larger, flatter village with numerous government departments.

After a long and tiring day, the doctor travelled through all the villages, including the highest area of Al-Soudah where the climate was noticeably colder compared to the village he worked in, which was surrounded by mountains and considered a warmer area in the Tihamia region.

That night, the doctor slept in a small manor owned by an elderly woman. She served him a simple meal of wheat and a small amount of ghee and provided him with a thin blanket. Despite the uncomfortable sleeping conditions, the exhaustion from his travels and perhaps the ghee helped him to fall into a deep sleep. He did not awaken until the sound of knocking on the door at dawn, when the elderly woman reminded him in a shrilled voice, "Perform ablution for the morning prayer, my son. May God protect you."

He woke up, tidied his bed, folded the blanket, and placed it on the pillow. He then went to the mosque, tied his mount outside, performed ablution and entered the mosque. He prayed two rak'ahs and joined a small group of no more than five people for the congregational prayer. Afterwards, he set out on his journey towards Abha.

The journey ahead was not too far, and as the doctor made his descent towards his destination, his mind was occupied with thoughts of his trip to Homs. The city that he was nearing reminded him of his first encounter with its gentle charm, the bustling shops, friendly locals and beautiful houses nestled in neighbourhoods that were home to a variety of nationalities. Despite the large number of people from diverse backgrounds, they were all united under the name "the people of Abha." This city had a unique ability to make strangers feel welcome and eliminate any sense of alienation, unlike other places where such barriers were common.

By pure coincidence, the doctor ran into an Egyptian

colleague working at Abha General Hospital, who insisted on hosting him in his home. It turned out that the fellow doctor's family had travelled to Cairo only three days beforehand. At first, he was reluctant to accept the invitation, but after some discussion, he agreed, and went with his colleague to the house, which was close to the hospital. Inside, he felt the warmth and presence of feminine touches that were left by the host's wife.

They discussed various topics, including scientific, political and cultural affairs, which brought great relief and overwhelming joy to our friend, who had missed such conversations in the village, which he began to feel more accustomed to. They also talked about their travel stories, particularly those to Aden, and some even further to Addis Ababa and Djibouti in Africa to purchase various goods such as clothes, perfumes and other items. Aden, due to its proximity, received most of the goods that were imported from Bombay, which was known for its diverse range of products. Although he was going to Syria, which didn't know hunger. There he spent time with friends and studied at all levels. He was not a reckless young man. That's why most of his friends and female colleagues, especially at the university level, were not impressed by him, due to his seriousness and strictness, which didn't fit the reckless spirit they wanted, and which modern life imposed. Despite his desire to indulge in some of the absurdities of youth, such as going to mixed cafes and cinemas, he was too serious, which did not fit their perception of him. He attributed his seriousness to his upbringing and family status, and instead directed his energy towards science and education. However, he felt apprehensive about traveling, even though he was slated to travel the next day to Jeddah and then on to Damascus. Before embarking on his journey, he planned to spend two days shopping for gifts for his family and close friends, taking advantage of the abundance of goods from all around the world. He was also impressed by the kindness, simplicity and generosity of the people he encountered, although he refrained from participating in some local customs such as smoking shisha while observing patrons at cafes sitting on woven chairs.

He purchased a few reasonably priced women's fabrics from the markets before returning to his modest hotel in the city centre to prepare for an early bedtime in anticipation of his journey to Damascus the following day. Sleep evaded him, as he was preoccupied with thoughts of his family and concerns about elder Jaber's marriage proposal. Although he had not met the bride or her family, elder Jaber spoke highly of them, citing their good character and reputation.

Upon arriving in Damascus and completing the airport formalities, he headed to the station to get the bus to his hometown of Homs. After waiting for an hour, the bus finally departed with its diverse passengers, en route to Homs, which was about 180 kilometres away from Damascus. He was amazed by the vast distance between the Tihami village, surrounded by mountains, and the Orontes River where he had spent most of his childhood and teenage years. Memories of the old neighbourhoods in Homs flooded his mind - the stone-paved streets, numerous shops and the rich historical aroma of ancient cities.

His family welcomed him with overwhelming affection and inquired about the Holy Land. He did his best to explain in detail, but his responses failed to satisfy their curiosity. To avoid disappointing them, he reluctantly resorted to silence and simply shook his head, indicating his reluctance to share his experiences.

Many of his family members were unaware that he resided in a small village located in the southern Tihama, while others only knew of the holy cities, Mecca and Medina. How can one explain something like that to the varying levels of knowledge and experiences that individuals possess. While one person's understanding of a particular subject may be broad and comprehensive, another's may be limited and narrow.

Over the course of three days, his family bombarded him with multiple questions in an attempt to gain a better understanding of his experiences, or maybe it was just the natural and acceptable human curiosity.

He retained vivid memories of every detail of his homeland - from the winding alleys to the familiar faces and delicious cuisine. However, despite his familiarity with his surroundings, his travels had imparted upon him a wealth of new knowledge and experiences, expanding his horizons and granting him fresh perspectives. Traveling, in and of itself, a thrilling experience. It is filled with the intoxicating fragrance of discovery, the beauty of poetry and the tantalising flavours of new cuisines. Despite his extensive exploration of his homeland and the nostalgia it evoked, he found himself overcome with a peculiar yearning for elder Jaber and the infirmary in the remote southern village. He reminisced about the tales of patients and their suffering that were recounted to him repeatedly. He had learned to listen to them with compassion, as though it was part of a psychological form of treatment.

He had made up his mind to inform his family of his decision to return to his place of work, using the excuse that his vacation was nearing its end. Later that evening, his mother disclosed to him that there was a bride who shone as bright as the moon. To her surprise, he did not share her enthusiasm, and his mother was taken aback by his lack of excitement. She then remarked, "At least you'll make your loneliness comfortable away from home." He chuckled and replied, "Loneliness?! I've never felt it." He could tell that his mother was not entirely pleased by his response, for she raised her eyebrows in surprise and said nothing, as if he had insulted her.

She left the room, her anger palpable, and when he departed from Homs for Damascus, she did not bid him farewell like the rest of the family.

Perhaps it was an act of silent protest. As he journeyed back to Damascus, he experienced a sense of joy that he could not explain or attribute to any particular source. While waiting at the Damascus airport to board his flight to Jeddah, he recalled a popular saying that he had heard from a woman in the Tihama dispensary. Even though there were no introductions made, he felt as if she were referring to him when she said, "I was happy in the country where I found happiness, not the country where I was born." He realised that this simple adage held a profound truth, one that the doctor firmly believed in. Often, our thoughts lead us astray from the truth, and we follow our whims instead.

Upon his arrival in Jeddah, the "Bride of the Red Sea," as it was affectionately called in the Hijaz and throughout the Kingdom, he still had more than a week left of his vacation. The idea of performing Umrah occurred to him, and since Mecca was nearby, he decided to pay a visit to the holy sanctuary. As he stood before the Holy Kaaba and performed his circumambulation, he felt an overwhelming sense of happiness.

He felt a sense of inner peace and contentment. Upon returning to Jeddah, he eagerly prepared for his next adventure to Abha in just two days' time. There, he met with his Egyptian friend, a doctor who, like himself, was still unmarried. The two stayed up late into the night, reminiscing about their respective hometowns and the people they had left behind. He spoke of Homs, and in particular, the persistent efforts of his mother to find him a suitable match. Despite their numerous attempts, he remained steadfast in his rejection of the idea.

As he made his way towards the village after an entire day of descent, he couldn't help but feel a sense of relief and excitement despite the long and tiring journey. He was grateful that his physical stamina held up and that he encountered no obstacles along the way. He arrived at his small house at the time of the Ishaa evening prayer. He unpacked his bag and arranged the gifts he had brought from Homs, mainly dessert dishes that the Levant region was known for. He took a cold shower and changed into his pyjamas, sinking into a deep, uninterrupted sleep until the call to prayer for Fajr woke him.

He was relieved that elder Jaber had not noticed his arrival, especially since he had come late at night and was exhausted from his travels.

The next morning, the villagers woke up to a sunless rainy day, and the valley that almost bisected the village overflowed with water. However, the sturdy stone buildings, which the villagers called "forts," were unscathed and remained standing throughout the years.

He made his way to the infirmary, eagerly anticipating the latest stories and gossip from the villagers, as well as their dreams and desires. His relationship with the locals was not merely based on his role as a doctor; it was a human connection where they shared their fears, obsessions and simple joys, even if it involved singing and dancing in the mountains, where the sound seemed to disappear into the sky, carried away by the clouds and the wind towards the sea.

Trees and plants bore their names, wells, fields, valleys and fortresses, as well as man.

Suddenly, in walked elder Jaber, announcing his arrival with his usual noise. His sharp voice, sense of humour and well-known laughter filled the room. Everyone in the village knew him and his story - the marriage that had preoccupied the entire village for a long time. Eventually, thoughts calmed down and the de facto matter was that love was the master of judgments, as he had married someone from a class he didn't belong to.

Without asking permission or even knocking, he barged into the doctor's room. But upon realising that the doctor was in the middle of examining a patient, he took a few steps back and closed the door quietly - something he wasn't used to doing. When the patient left, he knocked on the door and heard the doctor's voice saying, "Come on in, elder Jaber."

After greeting each other and catching up on family news and details of his long journey, the doctor laughed and said, "Glory be to God, you haven't changed, elder Jaber. Always rushing things. Let's talk more tonight on the rooftops since it's the middle of the month. "I swear by divorce, dinner is on me!" said elder Jaber. The doctor said furiously: "Didn't I advise you not to swear by divorce?"

Elder Jaber smiled and said, "Forgive me, I'll never do it again."

It was a night of utmost enjoyment, and the gentle breezes carried with them the scent of trees following the recent rain. The doctor was narrating the intricacies of his travels to elder Jaber and his ever-smiling wife, whose benevolent heart diffused joy throughout the room, despite her persistent attendance to the coffee, tea and dinner that she had so meticulously prepared. Her mastery in the culinary arts and kind demeanour had earned her recognition in the village.

The doctor was eager to hear news of the village and its inhabitants, particularly in regards to the subject of marriage, yet elder Jaber inundated him with inquiries about his journey since his arrival in Abha, followed by Jeddah, Mecca, Damascus and Homs. The doctor was a keen listener, his eyes enraptured by every detail he was presented, no matter how minor, as if he were experiencing an enthralling cinematic production.

At a late hour, elder Jaber's wife excused herself with a gracious smile and bid them goodnight. The doctor harboured a sense of optimism as he turned to his companion and tentatively posed the question, "Do you have any news?" However, elder Jaber's countenance became impassive, seemingly avoiding the topic of marriage that had surfaced in his absence. He did not offer comment, nor did he attempt to cause any discomfort. Nevertheless, the doctor understood that there was more to be said.

After a brief interval, he discerned that it was time to depart. He offered a smile as he bid his farewell and expressed his appreciation for the delightful evening, adding, "Please convey my gratitude to the hostess for the scrumptious dinner."

After a week of work at the infirmary, elder Jaber carried out his duties in an unusually quiet manner. He was a valuable asset to the dispensary for many reasons, including his familiarity with the villagers, both men and women, and his ability to keep their secrets and stories concealed from outsiders, even those from neighbouring villages with whom he shared a common ancestry. This sense of privacy and adherence to strict customs had been passed down through generations.

At the start of the following week, elder Jaber arrived as usual, speaking in a distinguished voice. When he found only the doctor, who was engrossed in a massive book, he greeted him before asking, "Doctor, do you want to hear some good news?" The doctor removed his glasses and turned towards elder Jaber, replying, "Of course! What is it?" Elder Jaber rubbed his palms together as he explained the news: the girl's brother returned from The Levant. The doctor understood that The Levant referred to the north, while Yemen referred to the south, so the brother could have been in one of the cities of Hijaz.

As for the topic of marriage, elder Jaber quickly responded, "I will explain all the details that have held me back since your return from traveling. The girl's uncles had rejected the idea of marrying outside the tribe, and her mother feared that she would suffer the pains of being a stranger in a distant land that no one knew anything about. Additionally, the girl was young and inexperienced. However, God granted her a chance through her brother, who had joined the army for three years in Jeddah. The brother was literate and showed signs of intelligence in his eyes. 'He lights up dark paths, as the jurists say.'" Elder Jaber turned to see the extent of his enthusiasm and found the doctor smiling. "Thank you for this incomplete good news."

Up until that moment, despite elder Jaber's elusive smile, the doctor was unsure of the purpose of their conversation. However, elder Jaber had promising news to share when he said, "You have to get to know him." The doctor shook his head in confusion, asking, "How is that possible when I do not know him and have never seen him before?"

Exactly one week later, elder Jaber entered the dispensary with his loud voice and well-known laugh. After greeting each other, the doctor was surprised when elder Jaber invited him to be his guest that night alongside a group of neighbours, including Ibn Hadi.

The doctor asked, "What is the occasion? And who is this Ibn Hadi that I'm hearing about for the first time?" Elder Jaber replied, "The occasion is your safe return from travel, and Ibn Hadi is the man who returned from the military and the brother of the girl." Then he winked, although no one was looking at him.

The doctor understood the situation and accepted the invitation, saying, "May God bless you."

That night was full of surprises. The guests were all elders of the village, yet the doctor did not feel like a stranger among them. He found that the returning soldier from the Hijaz was perhaps the closest to his world. He was different from the others in his knowledge and culture, which the doctor came to realise despite their kindness, generosity, character and appreciation for the stranger. The villagers protected him and checked on his wellbeing to ensure he did not feel alienated or far from his homeland. The soldier's council was close to the doctor, and he spoke well, with reverence and influence on those around him. It was a reverence refined by estrangement and knowledge of the other, then by the strict laws of the military, and finally by his constant search for knowledge through reading and learning. When the night was over, the returning soldier and the doctor became friends, due to their understanding and awareness of others. Three days after the invitation, elder Jaber's friend visited the doctor at the village dispensary. Just by chance, there were no patients, and they discussed various topics. He learned about the Syrian doctor's ancient family and their position in society.

The doctor found a sense of mutual satisfaction in the developing relationship between him and the family of his potential bride. They exchanged visits and the bond between them grew stronger. However, the doctor felt that the relationship was not complete, especially with the mother and father, who remained reserved despite their friendly smiles. The days passed in their usual cycle and with the slowness that characterised most villages. Strangely, the people of those villages seemed to enjoy this mundane pace, a pace that could only be perceived by those who came from a different place or left to another destination. Those individuals felt the difference and were haunted by the idea of leaving again and again, seeking a new experience and a wider world that would get rid of their attachment to that place and provide them with a broader perspective and an added experience.

As he travelled, his curiosity to discover the village with a new perspective grew. He read about its forts and farms and experienced the surprise of the silent torrent that appeared out of nowhere, spreading a mixture of joy and fear throughout the village. The emotional moment that accompanied the roar of the torrent descending from the distant mountains, where black clouds carried omens to the thirsty fields, brought with it strange and dissimilar stories.

Every mountain harbours secrets not meant for outsiders, while each mosque for the mountain people has a meaning beyond the usual religious rituals. The mountains themselves hold the secrets of the ancestors, with their songs evoking both sadness and goodness. In times of fear and panic, the mosque was the only place that issued orders for defence or attack, while in times of peace it served as the Shura Council for the villagers.

The doctor and his new friend developed a strong relationship through their frequent visits. Elder Jaber found this amusing and was pleased with the growth of their friendship. However, the doctor hadn't realised that his new friend was actually the brother of the girl whom elder Jaber had hoped would become his wife. Unfortunately, her mother was very strict and vehemently rejected the idea. The people in the mountainous region were known to be stubborn and insistent on their positions, even if they turned out to be wrong. The mother's overwhelming passion caused her to cling to two beliefs: first, that her daughter should not marry a stranger, even if he was educated and a doctor, as the young men in the village possessed qualities of manhood and courage. Second, that ultimately the doctor would return to his own country and family, and her daughter would have to accompany him to a strange and unfamiliar land, among strangers.

The father, on the other hand, took a more moderate position and put his faith in God to plan a good future for his daughter. He hoped that, even if she had to suffer from alienation and the sadness that comes with moving away from her village and friends, their innocent laughter would soon fill the place once again.

All of these events and opinions were discussed in secret between the strict mother and the more moderate father. The girl, on the other hand, remained in control of herself and her own desires. Her fondest memories were spent with her friends in the woods of the mountains, far from the village. It was as though she possessed complete freedom and the sweet anticipation of this time, which would start after

Fajr prayer and end around sunset. They would eat wheat bread and drink from the pure streams that permeated the mountains, increasing their enjoyment and anticipation of the forthcoming journey of joy and freedom that the family nurtured, as was customary in the mountain weather. Safety was assured, except for the occasional attack by wild animals.

After returning home, the girls excitedly shared their stories with their parents, who listened to the spontaneity with pleasure and saw the joy radiating from their eyes. The safety of the mountains was due to the absence of strangers and the familiarity between the villagers. The young men felt a sense of shame if they were to harm one of them, even if they were from a distant village. Despite this, innocent admiration and conversation still flowed between the young men and women, leaving an emotional impact on both parties.

In a hurry, Ibn Hadi visited the dispensary and asked his friend, the doctor, to accompany him to the neighbouring village market. He had important matters to discuss and was eager to change his surroundings and meet new faces.

The doctor agreed and, as the workload was usually light on market day, most of the villagers went there, leaving elder Jaber with only light medical duties to attend to.

After the Fajr prayer, they set off to the neighbouring village, not a great distance away, but they decided to rent two lively animals for the journey. Then they visited the manor of a well-known middle-aged woman whose husband had passed away not long ago, leaving her with a spacious house and large yard to accommodate the animals of her customers.

She served them a delicious breakfast of wheat bread, ghee and pure honey, and gave them the feeling she tended to the animals, providing them with water and fodder. In her sweet rustic dialect, she then offered them lunch, saying, "Stay a while, and you may have lunch."

Ibn Hadi thanked her for the delicious breakfast and declined her offer, stating that it would suffice them until dinner time. He then took out some money from his pocket to pay her, but she hesitated and said, "this time on me." He smiled and replied, "This is your livelihood and pension, you're woman of honour." When she was out of sight, the doctor expressed his confusion and said, "I did not understand, I thought you knew her previously." Ibn Hadi laughed and explained that the woman only opens her house to offer her services for halal livelihood, and that she even offers the option of staying overnight for a price. The doctor was amazed and remarked, "This kind of thing only happens in developed countries or perhaps in Damascus or Cairo." Ibn Hadi felt a sense of euphoria at the genuine praise.

They left the house and entered the bustling market, where the cacophony of sounds and movement never ceased. They made their purchases for their homes and, at the end of the market, found respite on a bench where fellow shoppers from neighbouring villages gathered seeking shade and rest. Memories and stories were shared amongst them. Suddenly, Ibn Hadi broached a sensitive topic: "Elder Jaber spoke to my parents about your desire to marry my only sister and relayed my father's hesitation and mother's refusal. Do you really want to marry her?"

The doctor was taken aback, his face flushing with confusion and surprise, as he held Ibn Hadi in the highest regard. Despite the doctor's confusion, Ibn Hadi waited patiently for an answer, seeking only the truth.

The doctor struggled to regain his composure, taking time to collect his thoughts and emotions. As he gazed upon Ibn Hadi's calm countenance, he sensed the expectation of an honest response, unclouded by sentiment or concern.

Finally, with the same tranquillity that imbued Ibn Hadi, he replied: "Believe me, elder Jaber mentioned a woman, but did not name her. I only learned of her connection to you just now, from you personally. I'm happy to hear she's your sister."

"May God decree good for you both," he said. The doctor felt relieved as he gazed at the familiar features of Ibn Hadi and found that his attitude was the same as before. They returned to their separate conversation without broaching the subject of marriage. As the market drew to a close and the men and women dispersed to their respective villages, the marketplace returned to its previous state of calm, waiting for the following week's activities. Overwhelmed by a sense of serenity and the impact of change, they made their way towards their nearby village.

Upon arriving home, they agreed to schedule a future appointment. The doctor found it difficult to sleep as he felt an initial sense of alienation, which quickly dissipated. Nothing occurred that warranted amplifying their normal and logical conversation, particularly given Ibn Hadi's rightful concern for his spoiled sister, who was the recipient of the family's love and affection. Acknowledging the fluidity and spontaneity of what had happened, he accepted the course of events with ease.

The following day, the rain poured heavily, causing the water level in the valley to rise to unprecedented heights.

People stayed indoors, and the marketplace in the village quieted, with only a few shops daring to open for a few hours in the hopes of making a profit.

For three consecutive days and nights, the rain fell incessantly, causing the village elders to gather in the mosque and discuss the plight of the residents and the poor. Two villagers were tasked with inspecting old houses that were at risk of collapsing due to the rain. On the fourth day, the sun finally emerged, and people returned to their work and trade. The village was once again filled with pleasant scents, and the people rejoiced, singing in the fields and grazing the animals in the mountains.

The doctor did not see his friend Ibn Hadi for an entire week, but received updates through elder Jaber. He was visited by a group of patients who had been unable to see him during the rainy days. One day, elder Jaber brought news that filled the doctor with joy. "Ibn Hadi sends his warmest regards and invites you to visit him after the Isha prayer tomorrow," he said.

The doctor exclaimed with joy, "May God bless you and him. I will be there on time, God willing."

The following day, after finishing his evening shift, he made his way to the "fort," as they call it, which consisted of four floors. Ibn Hadi and his family resided on the top floor, while the other three floors were occupied by different families from the village.

As Ibn Hadi received the doctor in his reception, his manly composure radiated from his eyes and his "al-Jimma," the long hair that reached his shoulders, added to his bold appearance. Upon entering the council, he found the father seated at the front, wearing a white veil and a headband adorned with two branches of freshly harvested basil. The father welcomed him warmly and expressed his admiration, "My son speaks highly of you and praises your knowledge and morals. You are one of us, among the people of this village, and hundreds of people welcome you."

The doctor expressed his gratitude and responded, "I appreciate your kindness and generosity. I understand the morals of the people in this village, and I feel as though I am one of you."

As customary, the initial conversations revolved around sharing memories, particularly the doctor's experiences during his study days in The Levant.

The father remarked, "Syria was famous for its agriculture and many other good things. Syrian women were known for their delicious and diverse cuisine."

In vain, he waited for the conversation to move into another subject other than food. Ibn Hadi tried to change the course of conversation, but he couldn't interrupt his father's talk.

There fell a long silence, and then the father turned to the doctor with a curious look on his face. "Doctor, may I ask if you have ever been married?" he inquired. The doctor, feeling a bit taken aback, shook his head to indicate that he had not been married. Ibn Hadi and the doctor both felt embarrassed by the sudden question, but the father sat up straight and a smile appeared on his face.

After the doctor left, Ibn Hadi asked his father, "Why did you embarrass our guest by asking about marriage? Is there something about him that concerns you?"

His father turned around and placed his green veil and basil next to him before sitting up to meet his son's gaze. "Son," he said, "your sister is growing older every day and she has not yet found her destined partner. I have thought a lot about what Jaber said, and I fear that if this doctor, whom I do not know and whose family I have never met, were to propose to her, people would talk. Your opinion is what I trust the most now, particularly after I found out that he comes from a great family and that he has a medical degree, which guarantees him a bright future and good income. Your mother is exerting a great deal of pressure and is rejecting the idea from the outset. I have been unable to convince her and, out of respect for our long-standing relationship, I will back off for now and look for another opportunity to bring up the subject. However, I know it is useless. But, since she loves you and values your opinion, I suggest you speak with her. Perhaps you can find a way to persuade her to agree to the idea."

His son nodded in agreement and said, "May God decree what is best for us all."

Time passed slowly, and there were no new developments on the matter. Even elder Jaber had stopped talking about the marriage, neither positively nor negatively. As for Ibn Hadi, he was aware of his mother's stubbornness and her desire to assert her dominance in the family.

The son, suddenly realising his newfound influence in the family, was struck by a bold idea. He knew that his mother held his aunt in high esteem due to her influential personality, not only within the family, but also in the village. His mother's sister was renowned for her unwavering determination and her voice that carried weight, even to her own sister, who completely rejected the idea of the marriage. It was then that a plan sprouted in the son's mind - to convince his aunt to consider the doctor a suitable partner. He would explain the doctor's excellent reputation in their community, his strong morals and extensive knowledge.

He made his way to his aunt's home, which was not far away. He greeted her, kissing her head. The fragrance of caddis and basil filled the air as she greeted him warmly. He took a seat on one of the benches and she regaled him with tales and stories, not giving him a chance to speak. She was known in the village as the "gossip," and he couldn't help but chuckle at this moniker, hoping she wouldn't notice. He knew that if she did, he would be in trouble without any way to make amends.

In a moment of sudden silence on her part, he took the initiative to say, "Oh aunt, I have some information that I would like to share with you." She replied, "tell me, my son. May it be good news." "God willing, it is good news, and it concerns our small family. When I returned from the Hijaz, I missed my village so much, especially its simple and sincere people, its mountains and valleys, the scent of its plants, and the echoes of its mountains that reflect the continuous state of love without disruption or retreat."

It was as if Ibn Hadi was planning to win her approval of the idea of marrying outside the village and tribe with this emotional introduction. Her word held great influence within the family, village and tribe, without any hesitation or hypocrisy. Her decision was definitive, and she would never retreat or escape from the truth that she believed in and would fiercely defend it if necessary. .

When she allowed him to go on, as he spoke honestly about his sister and her future, he was attempting to persuade his aunt to consider the distant future, and that going to Abha was not a far-fetched dream and would not change anything in the matter, considering that the world is more spacious and presents the most beautiful opportunity for learning about others.

A strange silence prevailed on her part, with cautious anticipation on his part. She let out a sigh and said, "Your words, my son, are extremely sincere." At that moment, he felt a mixture of joy and anticipation. This woman, who was filled to the core with honesty and love, didn't know evasion or lying, but rather, she was like a blank sheet of paper.

"My dear son, for girls, marriage is a significant milestone that one day they will inevitably reach, whether the destined partner comes from within or outside the village. It is a destiny that is written for all of us."

Upon hearing this, the son felt confident that his plan would succeed, and his aunt would help convince his mother to change her mind. His aunt turned to him and asked, "Who is lucky enough to propose to the most beautiful girls in the village?" The son hesitated for a moment, but the aunt urged him to speak, her tone reminiscent of an experienced interrogator. Eventually, the son turned to face her and said, "The Syrian doctor." He uttered these words like a bombshell, causing a heavy and deadly silence to settle between them.

The aunt soon let out a deep sigh and said, "May God

write happiness and goodness for her in the coming days, she deserves all the best." Although she did not explicitly state it, the son felt reassured that she had come to accept the reality of the situation. He kissed her head and said, "Keep well, Aunt," before hurriedly leaving with joy filling his heart.

The next day, his aunt visited them and spent a long time alone with her sister. He was with his father, who was preparing for a business trip to Aden to buy some goods that they sold in their village and nearby villages, such as fabrics, gold and silver jewellery, and various goods bought by men and women, as well as cardamom, coffee and spices coming from East Asia.

Throughout the night, the camel caravan was getting ready for the seasonal trip in two days, as they did every year. His father asked him, "What do you think about the idea of marriage? If I come back and there's a good match for you, may Allah bless her, I'm open to the idea. But, at the same time, I'm worried about the upcoming separation, which is unavoidable. The doctor will definitely go back to his homeland one day, and her religious duty will be to accompany him wherever he goes."

Ibn Hadi rarely left the house and became close to his sister. She provided him with reassurance and confided in him about her dreams and aspirations. In her childhood, she also learned to read and write, which opened up new worlds beyond her familiar surroundings of friends, mountains, firewood and valleys. She committed their names to memory.

The journey to Aden typically took several weeks, barring any adverse weather conditions such as rain, dust, or the rare bandit encounter. Despite these risks, the travellers took comfort in their familiarity with the established and secure routes used by other caravans from various tribes. These experienced travellers offered invaluable advice and guidance on the potential obstacles and hazards they may encounter along the way. This accumulated knowledge served as a free guide to help ensure the safety of the convoy, as safety was the first and final consideration in the convoy's law, from its departure until its safe return.

Ibn Hadi anxiously counted the passing nights and days, eagerly awaiting his father's safe return. He shared this same sense of anticipation with the village doctor, who received updates on the father's well-being from his patients, and from elder Jaber, a trusted informant who kept his wife and the doctor informed about the goings-on in the village, including its secrets and stories. After approximately a month and a half, a renowned camel rider, known for conveying messages and secret stories, informed the villagers that the caravan would arrive in two days and that he had seen them in excellent condition. The news quickly spread throughout the village, and the women expressed their joy by ululating, dispelling the anxiety that had gripped them all, for every household, regardless of size, had a relative among the caravan's members.

The camel rider was correct. Two days later, the caravan gradually emerged from the distance, accompanied by the sound of gunfire from all directions of the village, as if it were a grand wedding celebration. The doctor emerged from his home, witnessing the overwhelming joy that transformed the once-quiet village into a symphony of women's and men's voices and gunfire, which continued until the convoy had arrived in its entirety. Even the camels seemed to share in the jubilation with their groans.

The forts overlooking the valley were adorned with the silhouettes of women searching for their loved ones - husbands, relatives, lovers or sons. This poignant scene was repeated several times a year, evoking both fear and joy in the village. The doctor was deeply moved by the resilience of the men and the enduring love of the women, akin to the hardy trees that thrived on the slopes of towering mountains during times of drought and famine.

His admiration and affection for the village and its inhabitants only grew stronger. After a couple of hours, the gunshots and camel groans ceased, and the women retreated from the windows. Each man returned to his home for a peaceful slumber, revelling in the comforting thought "there's no place like home." The lights in the houses flickered off one by one, leaving only the sound of rustling leaves in the air.

Two weeks after the return of the convoy, the doctor requested a private meeting with elder Jaber. However, Jaber declined the suggestion of holding the meeting at the dispensary and instead proposed that they convene at his home, where the presence of Um Jaber could facilitate a more candid discussion. The idea was accepted, and the conversation revolved around the topic of marriage. It was agreed that Ibn Hadi would be fully informed of the details, including elder Jaber's intention to speak on behalf of the doctor. Despite his fondness for jesting, Jaber was recognised as one of the village's esteemed elders, renowned for his wisdom.

Two days after their initial meeting, the trio had an appointment with the girl's father. Elder Jaber acted as the mediator for the doctor and assured him that they could overcome any obstacles and come to a satisfactory agreement with the mother, who opposed the marriage. The doctor nodded in agreement and waited for two days until Jaber informed him that the meeting was scheduled for the following night after the evening prayer at the father's home. Ibn Hadi insisted that his aunt and her silent husband be present, as her dominant personality made people deal with her cautiously and respectfully. It seemed as though her husband had known the message for a long time, so he resorted to silence and the choice of safety.

During the meeting, they enjoyed a meal of popular dishes, including roasted meet with herbs, squash and various fruits, followed by coffee and tea. The father began by offering prayers and reciting blessings for the Prophet, before addressing the matter that elder Jaber had presented on behalf of the Syrian doctor, who had become a valued member of the village and had expressed his desire to marry their daughter. The father praised the doctor's virtues, including his generosity, high moral standards, and excellent education, as well as his esteemed family background. In principle, he blessed the union and wished them all the success and happiness in their new life. At that moment, the sound of a woman's voice could be heard ululating, expressing happiness and triumph. However, inside the room where the sounds of joy were coming from, there was a woman who was crying, as a sign of rejection and defeat, after the father's agreement. Another woman was also present, a young girl who was unaware of the unknown and uncertain future that lay ahead.

In an attempt to regain some of her power, and amidst her tears, the woman turned towards the father and said, "If you are still insistent on marrying your daughter to a stranger, then I have one condition." The father turned towards her, hiding a smile and said, "Tell me your condition, and I promise to fulfil it." She wiped away her tears with the edge of her scarf and lowered her head, as if she was deep in thought, tapping her index finger on the mat and saying, "I want you to organise a wedding unlike any other in our village or the neighbouring villages." The father replied, "Everyone agrees, there's no objection to that."

The following day, Ibn Hadi visited the infirmary and saw elder Jaber. Afterwards, he entered the doctor's office, who received the blessing of the father, and the mother, albeit reluctantly. Ibn Hadi expressed their concerns about parting with their only daughter, whether in Abha or anywhere else. The doctor assured him, "Believe me, I will ensure that she lives as if she were among you."

Later, Ibn Hadi returned home and met with his family to discuss the wedding date, dowry and other related matters. The conversation proceeded calmly, with Ibn Hadi directing his attention towards his mother to avoid any further complications or unreasonable requests. His aunt was also present during these meetings, acting as a tool of pressure that his mother could not resist. The mother faced her problems with a broken spirit, escaping to cry alone where no one could see her, even though she didn't want that either. She felt defeated and weak. However, life's experiences, both negative and positive, have the power to reshape a person, to allow them to create a new version of themselves, refined by trials, sadness and joy.

After several weeks, the doctor surprised everyone with the news of his impending move to Abha and the arrival of another doctor to take his place. Despite his mixed emotions, he felt a strong attachment to the people of the village, who he had grown to love as if he were one of their own. However, he knew that even a small city like Abha had everything a person could need, and he wouldn't have to wait for the weekly market to buy essentials.

Everyone was surprised, including elder Jaber, who was struck by the news, feeling hurt that the doctor hadn't confided in him earlier, "Why didn't you tell me earlier? I'm your closest friend!" The doctor felt pained at the thought of leaving his friends and thanked them for the depth of their friendship,

"I'm now one of you, and I will return to visit and remain a part of your community." The father wished him success and happiness, reminding him that Abha was not too far away.

As everyone dispersed, a sudden hush fell over the doctor's home. In that stillness, memories of Homs flooded his mind – its winding streets and its people. Though he couldn't explain why, he felt a sense of fleeting sorrow, a legitimate and humane emotion that he knew would eventually fade away. That night, he tried to pass the time by reading, but found himself unable to focus. Instead, he lay in bed, thinking of elder Jaber and all the stories he would miss hearing.

He only managed to sleep at dawn after he had finished his prayers and finally drifted into a deep sleep. The next day was a welcome break, affording him the precious time he needed to sort through his clothes and numerous scientific books. He carefully packed away a selection of Egyptian magazines, which he planned to leave for his friend Ibn Hadi, an avid reader with an insatiable appetite for knowledge. He also gathered up a collection of Arabic cultural publications from Dar Al-Hilal, as well as translated novels and international plays. This gift was like a testimony of friendship and an encouragement to read more and discover the world of reading, with all its wonder and amazement that never ceases.

In preparation for his move to Abha in a month's time, the doctor had made an agreement with his trusted friend and confidant, Ibn Hadi, to delay their marriage plans until he had started his new job and secured a rental property. News of the Syrian doctor's forthcoming marriage to a local girl quickly spread throughout the village, sparking many conversations and debates on the rooftops as people sought respite from the heat. Surprisingly, the majority of the supporters were women, leading some to speculate whether the doctor's union was a way to gain the freedom and mobility that only men had traditionally enjoyed on their travels to Aden, Mogadishu and Ma'su, or if it was simply fuelled by jealousy and envy among the women themselves.

After a month had passed, the doctor moved into a small house located in the village district, situated in close proximity to the hospital where he worked. He rented the entire house and set about making preparations for his wedding ceremony, which was to be held in the village. However, he soon found himself facing a dilemma when it came to navigating the local customs and traditions. Unsure of how to proceed, he turned to the only person who could help him - the experienced elder Jaber, who possessed a wealth of knowledge about the village and its secrets.

On the first day when he arrived, the doctor went straight to the house of elder Jaber. Jaber's wife greeted him warmly and welcomed him inside, explaining that her husband was "out buying some items for the house." As they conversed, the wife appeared somewhat nervous, her eyes glancing towards the window by the door. Just then, Jaber emerged in front of the door. She opened the door for him saying in a loud voice "the doctor is here." Jaber welcomed him saying: "your presence is a wonderful delight", asking about his health and his experiences in Abha so far. The doctor briefly recounted his experiences, but soon revealed his main concern: the upcoming marriage. He felt overwhelmed by the customs and procedures of marriage in the village, such as the dowry, the clothes and the types of jewellery. Jaber listened patiently and reassured him that everything would be taken care of smoothly and with calm thinking.

Meanwhile, the prospective wife was lost in deep thought. She cherished her village, its mountains and the earthy aroma of its plants. But from time to time, she would dream of a new life in far-off lands, filled with new experiences and people. This idea slowly but surely grew on her, painting a picture of a life beyond the familiar scents of her village. Perhaps her future husband would teach her how to read and write, or introduce her to religious studies like the Quran and Hadith. Maybe she would even learn new cooking styles. As these thoughts filled her mind, she couldn't help but wonder about the life that lay ahead of her.

Is this a simple dream of hers, or a deep-seated desire that she thinks about as she watches her brother read? Where does the pleasure that illuminates his eyes come from, and what brings him such happiness and joy after he finishes reading and closes the book's pages? When will I ever experience this feeling?

She posed a question to herself that she did not yet know the answer to, but she was certain that one day she would find out. Perhaps the husband whom God sent from The Levant to their mountainous village would be the one to unlock the door to reading, writing and the joy she witnessed in her brother.

Normally, she may have chuckled at these thoughts, which dwelt in the realm of the unknown. However, one day, she noticed her mother's unusually joyous demeanour, and her smile brought back a long-absent sense of happiness to the household that had been lost due to the mother's stance on marrying a stranger who was not from their village or the neighbouring ones.

Life changes without us even realising it, and as such, our psyche, moods and worldview are in a constant state of flux, perpetually shifting and never ceasing. This is the human soul, laden with contradictions, traversing the world with laughter and tears simultaneously.

Taking advantage of her mother's newfound happiness, she asked her, "What is a wedding about?" While gazing out the window at the rain, smelling the various fragrances it carried.

Her mother turned her body toward her daughter, her love for her emanating differently. "It is like the union between God's creations and those who marry, every day; it is life and its eternal law."

The bride's countenance remained unchanged despite her mother's vague response, but she forced a smile to show her gratitude. Her mother then asked, "Are there any questions on your mind regarding marriage and its secrets?"

The bride lifted the tresses of hair that obscured her youthful face with her palm and said without fear or hesitation: "I have a friend who is older than us and divorced, who used to graze the animals with us, and her talk captivated those who listened to her. One time, she told us tales of a woman named Zafira, who lived in a distant mountain. The story sent shivers down our spines, and she never repeated it again. But if it was true, the story left us questioning the idea of marriage!

We feared that this story had spread from mountain to mountain, winding through the oak trees rooted in the earth for hundreds of years, passed down by our ancestors and carried on the tongues of people during the dark nights on the mountain tops. Nights that tempted them to pluck a star that twinkled from the sky, only to find it had already disappeared into the vast eternity that extended beyond sight."

The mother continued to smile, observing the emotions that flickered across her child's face. Her daughter's mature and healthy appearance revealed the wisdom exuding for her brown face, garnered from the mountains, where the scent of trees and the songs of the earth harmonised with the echoes of human voices and the monologues of passing clouds, heading to other mountains, and singing different songs.

The mother's mind drifted, but she suddenly noticed her daughter, as if she were seeing her for the first time. She laughed heartily and exclaimed, "You're mad!" Then she asked her daughter, "What is the story of Zafira, the mountain girl?"

Her daughter settled into her seat and removed a string of basil from her dark hair. She then began to speak, saying, "May God bless you, daughter of Ahmad. Here is the story that the married woman told us, as if she was revealing a dangerous secret."

"She left her village early in the morning, with her house perched above the valley filled with fig trees. It was the reason why she woke up so early - to pick the ripe figs, which she ate with her usual breakfast of wheat or barley bread that she disliked, but could not refuse. She was weaker than her siblings, with a thin body that made it hard for her to decline anything.

Her family called her Zafira, after her aunt who was more

masculine in both shape and demeanour, unlike her. Zafira was only seventeen years old and uneducated, as schooling was only for boys in the village. Life in the village was monotonous, with little changing day-to-day.

One winter morning, Zafira's mother whispered to her that her sister, Azza, would be in charge of grazing the animals. Her mother left before Zafira could respond, leaving her waiting in the family's home. Eventually, her mother entered with an unusual smile and hugged her tightly, smelling of Paris Nights perfume mixed with basil, wazab and kadi.

'I have good news for you,' her mother said, lifting Zafira's face with her hands. 'A groom has come for you.' Joy, fear, and sadness all welled up inside Zafira. She thought of her beloved sheep in Wadi al-Tin, who would undoubtedly miss her. Tears streamed down her face, and her mother reassured her, 'Tears of joy, God willing, you will be happy, oh Zafira.'

As the wedding approached, Zafira couldn't help but cry. The groom was old and had married many times before, which only added to her sadness and depression. But there was no escape. On the night of the wedding, her mother gave her a new pair of trousers with a belt made of a strong that couldn't be removed easily. The wedding went as her mother had planned, but the groom struggled to untie her trousers and eventually had to use a dagger to cut the rope. Zafira screamed, and ululation came from outside the room. The groom reassured her and left for the night.

Years later, Zafira's daughter asked her about this ritual of marriage, and Zafira's mind wandered back to the memories of her own wedding. She laughed with her daughter, glad that the ritual had passed. Zafira rarely left her home, fearing gossip, but she longed to visit the mountains where she could indulge her love of plants and trees."

Elder Jaber asked the doctor if his dowry was ready, and he nodded. Elder Jaber then asked how much it was, to which the doctor replied between five hundred and a thousand. Elder Jaber had other requests, which he would explain later, including various types of clothing, silver, belts and rings that a woman could wear.

"Tomorrow, we will meet in the infirmary, and I will inform you of what remains to be done," he said, bidding farewell as they parted ways. The doctor couldn't sleep that night, consumed with worry. He woke early, foregoing his usual amount of rest, and headed to the infirmary. To his surprise, he found the brother of his bride-to-be waiting in the reception area. The man was greeted warmly with open arms and a broad smile.

The idea of marriage was an emotional transformation that brought a mother and daughter closer together. The mother knew her daughter was leaving their mountain village, the only home she'd ever known, for the city. She watched her daughter struggle with emotions, fighting back tears. But the mother, sensing her daughter's distress, turned a blind eye and offered her advice. "You are entering a new and unfamiliar society. Do your best to hide your weaknesses. Lean on your husband, whom fate has chosen to protect and love you." Her daughter listened, her mother's words coming from a place of experience and love.

Her father's face remained stoic, hiding a deep sadness that he didn't want his daughter to see. He smiled at the wedding guests, hoping that this new journey would bring his daughter joy, even if it would lead to a distance between them. Life was full of contradictions, and emotions could shift in an instant, but on this day, peace and happiness shone through.

The wedding party was a noisy affair, with gunshots ringing out and women ululating from open windows. The festivities continued throughout the day, with hospitality and various items prepared by men and women alike. Dancing and celebration carried on into the evening until the Maghrib call to prayer, leaving each person with a happy memory to hold onto.

The girls were eagerly anticipating their dreams for the future and waiting for their future partners, while also feeling saddened by the departure of their joyful and always-smiling friend. They prayed for her well-being, love and a reunion in the future.

In the village, which was nestled amidst the hills, the mother and daughter bid farewell, shedding tears that left the husband feeling confused and sad, not knowing how to console them. Meanwhile, the father, brother and uncle attempted to leave the emotional scene.

After the farewell, the husband and wife set off on their journey, first stopping at Abha through Al-Suda Mountain before traveling to Jeddah three days later by car. Prior to departure, she shyly requested that her husband perform Umrah, and he agreed.

On the plane to Damascus, she was overcome with extreme fear, trembling and crying, oblivious to her husband's attempts to reassure her with a smile. He comforted her, stating that it was just because it was her first time, and that she would eventually grow accustomed to future flights.

Although her fear subsided once the plane stabilised, she remained holding her husband's hand tightly, as if it were a lifeline she could not afford to lose.

Fortunately, the flight was smooth throughout, but her panic returned during the gradual descent and upon landing. Her husband smiled and reassured her, "We've arrived safely."

Although she felt shy and embarrassed, his comforting smile somewhat reassured her, and she returned it with a shy smile.

She found herself in an unfamiliar city with people speaking a dialect she didn't understand and customs she wasn't familiar with. Her husband tried to explain what was difficult for her to comprehend, and gradually, she began to assimilate. Nevertheless, she missed her village, nestled in the valley, surrounded by mountains and clouds.

One night, her husband heard her crying and screaming, "Oh God, how far away you are, oh south!"

He embraced her tightly and whispered, "We'll go back someday." Although this was a dream, she looked forward to every year, it faded and became distant after having children. However, her village, family and friends never forgot her.

Her life had taken her through various situations, and she had changed over time, even merging her accent with the Syrian dialect to speak a third language. Only her husband noticed this, smiling without comment so as not to upset her while she was far from home and family.

* * *